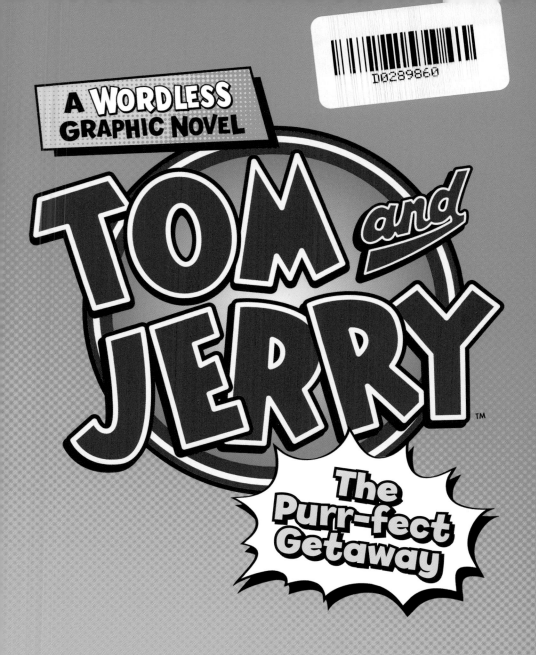

A WORDLESS GRAPHIC NOVEL

TOM and JERRY ™

The Purr-fect Getaway

by
**Christopher Harbo
& Scott Jeralds**

PICTURE WINDOW BOOKS
a capstone imprint

Published by Picture Window Books, an imprint of Capstone.
1710 Roe Crest Drive
North Mankato, Minnesota 56003
www.capstonepub.com

Library of Congress Cataloging-in-Publication Data
Names: Harbo, Christopher L., author. | Jeralds, Scott, illustrator.
Title: The purr-fect getaway / by Christopher Harbo ; illustrated by
   Scott Jeralds.
Other titles: Perfect getaway
Description: North Mankato, Minnesota : Picture Window Books, an
   imprint of Capstone, [2021] | Series: Tom and Jerry wordless graphic
   novels | Audience: Ages 5-7. | Audience: Grades K-1. | Summary: In a
   nearly wordless beginning graphic novel, house cat Tom's dreams of
   a peaceful Hawaiian vacation are shattered when Jerry the mouse
   pops out of his suitcase at the airport.
Identifiers: LCCN 2020038024 (print) | LCCN 2020038025 (ebook) |
   ISBN 9781515882770 (hardcover) | ISBN 9781515883715
   (paperback) | ISBN 9781515892441 (pdf) | ISBN 9781515892694
   (kindle edition)
Subjects: LCSH: Graphic novels. | CYAC: Graphic novels. | Airports-
   Fiction. | Vacations—Fiction. | Cats—Fiction. | Mice—Fiction. | Stories
   without words.
Classification: LCC PZ7.7.H36513 Pur 2021 (print) | LCC PZ7.7.H36513
   (ebook) | DDC 741.5/973—dc23
LC record available at https://lccn.loc.gov/2020038024
LC ebook record available at https://lccn.loc.gov/2020038025

Designer: Brann Garvey

Printed and bound in the USA.   3837

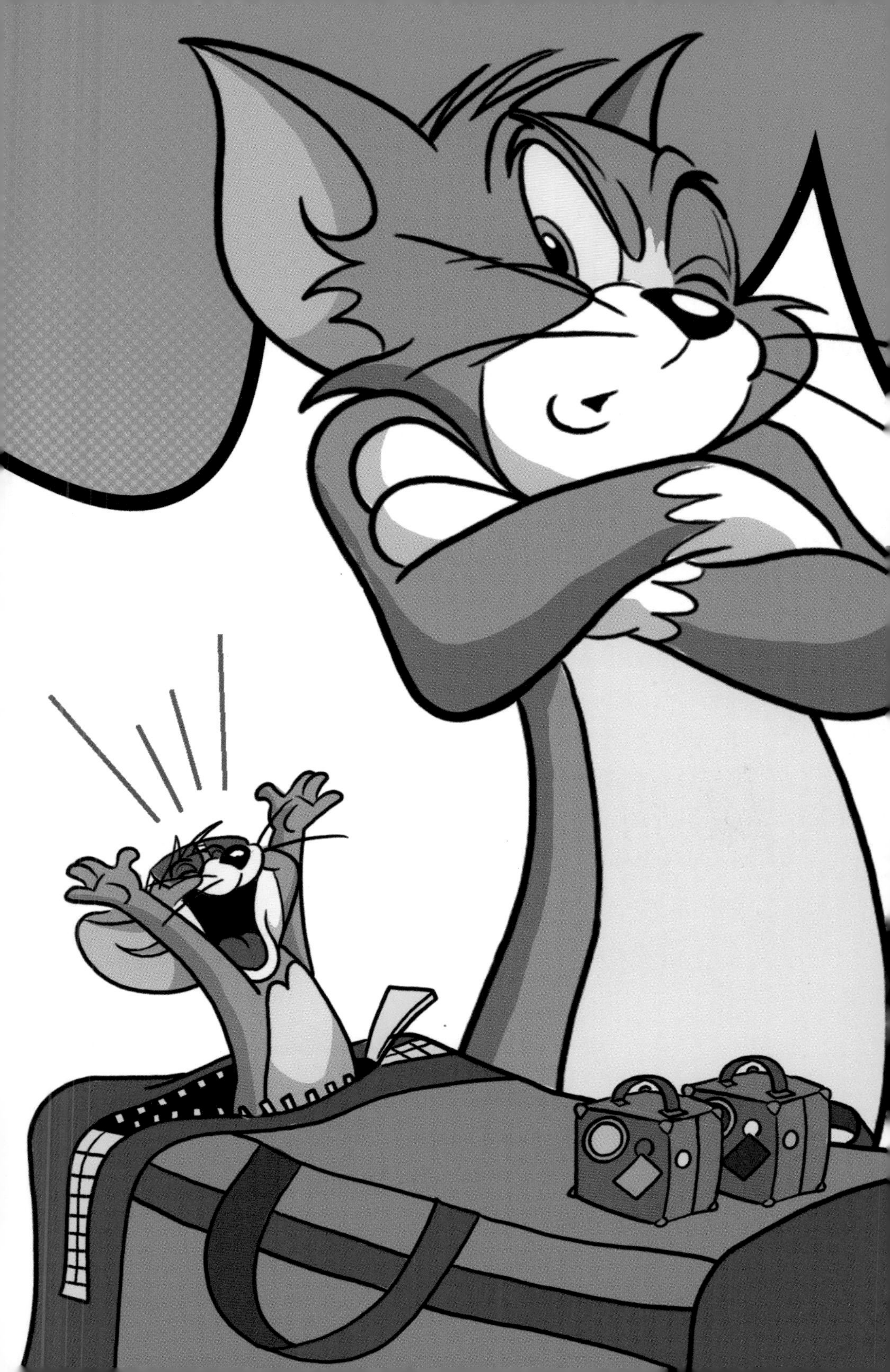

Meet TOM and JERRY™

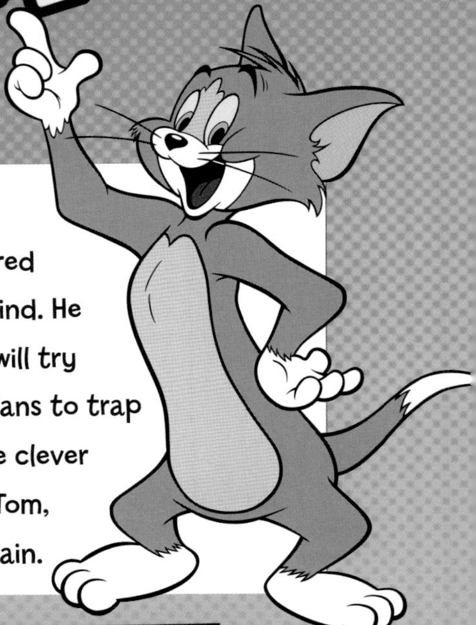

Tom Cat

Tom is a gray and white short-haired house cat with one thing on his mind. He wants to catch Jerry Mouse and will try anything to succeed! But Tom's plans to trap Jerry rarely work out. Instead, the clever mouse often turns the tables on Tom, leaving him with more pain than gain.

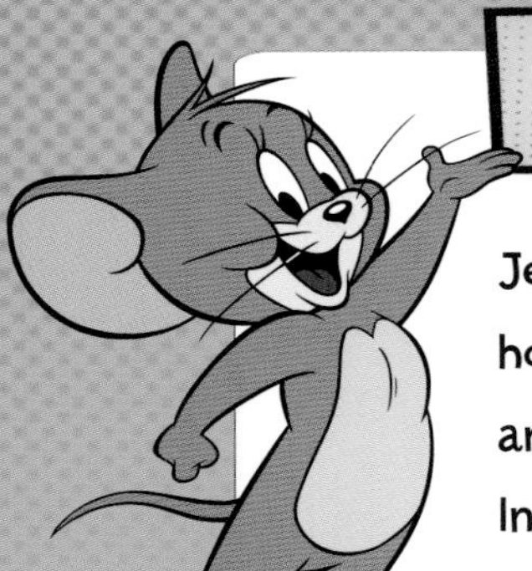

Jerry Mouse

Jerry is a brown mouse who lives in Tom's house. He may be tiny, but Jerry's strength and smarts are more than a match for Tom. In fact, Jerry takes great pride in teasing and outsmarting the cat at every turn.

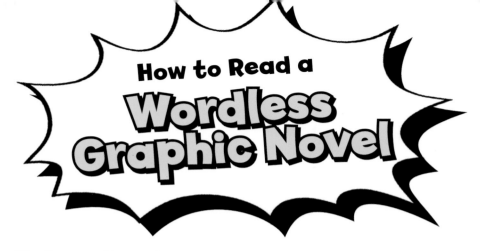

How to Read a Wordless Graphic Novel

Wordless graphic novels are easy to read. Boxes called panels show you how to follow the story. Look at the panels from left to right and top to bottom. Read any sound effects as you go.

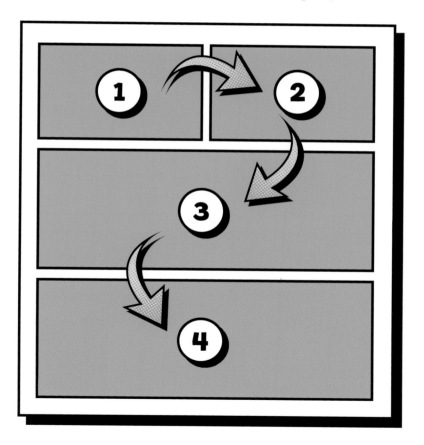

By putting the panels together, you'll understand the whole story!

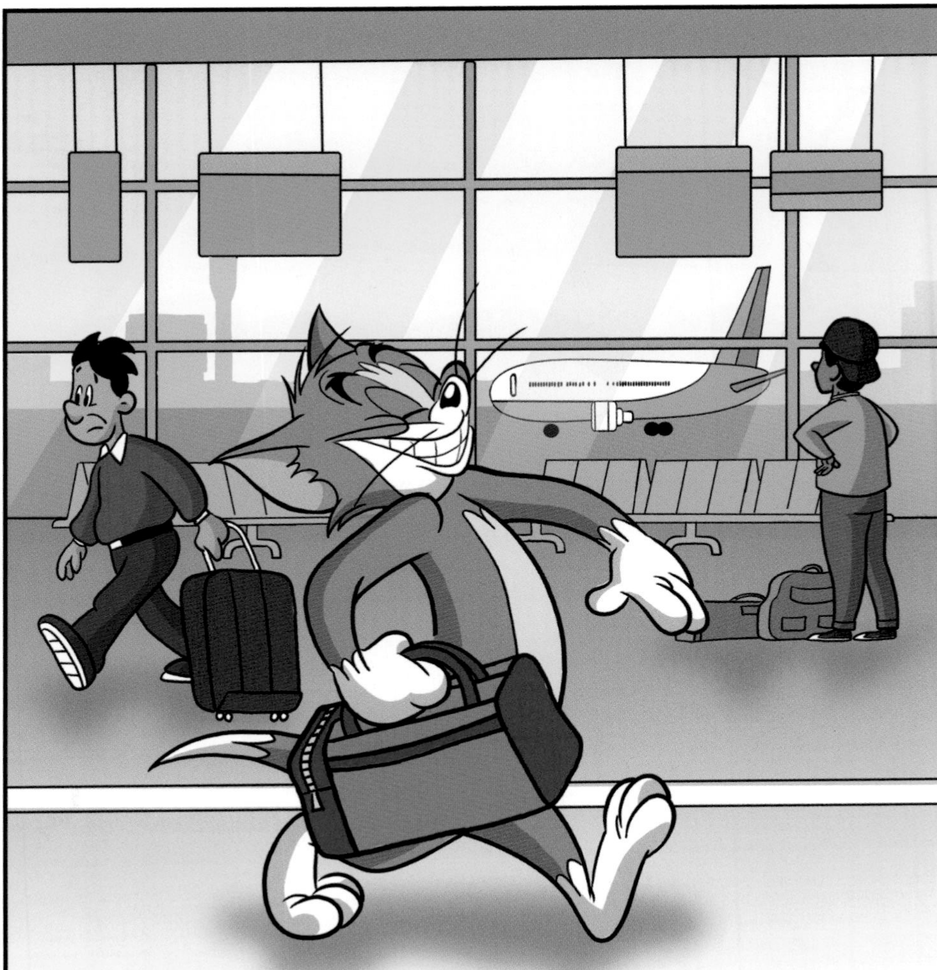

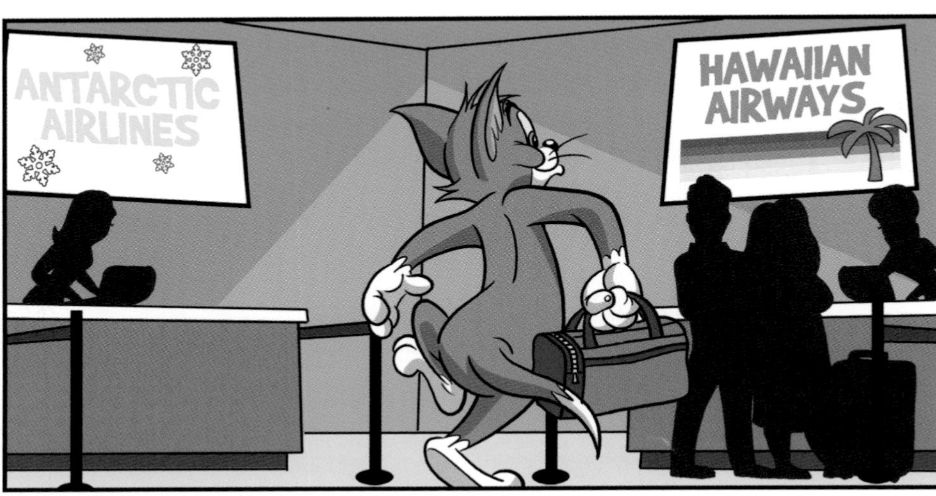
ANTARCTIC
AIRLINES
HAWAIIAN
AIRWAYS

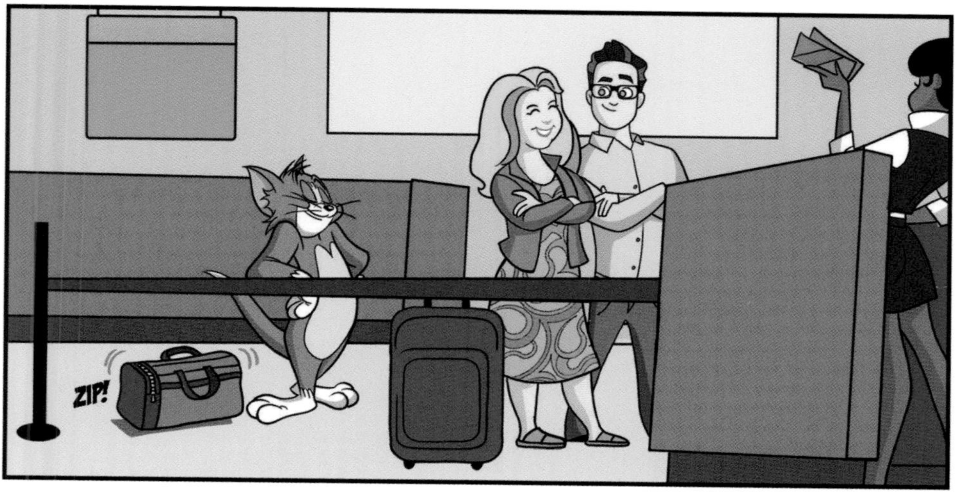
ZIP!

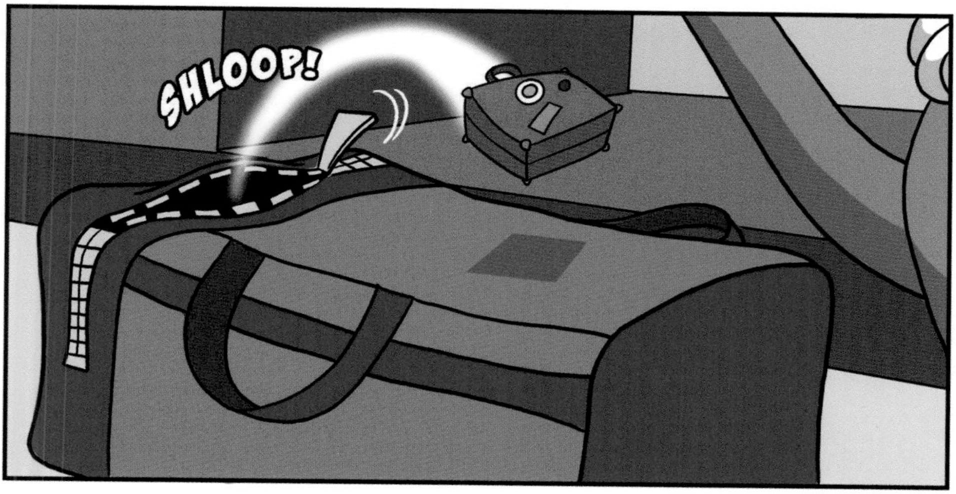
SHLOOP!

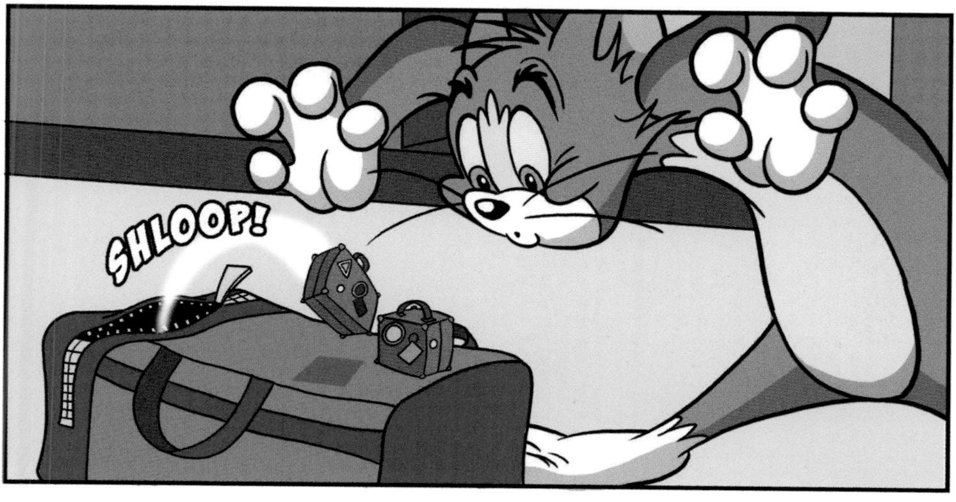
SHLOOP!

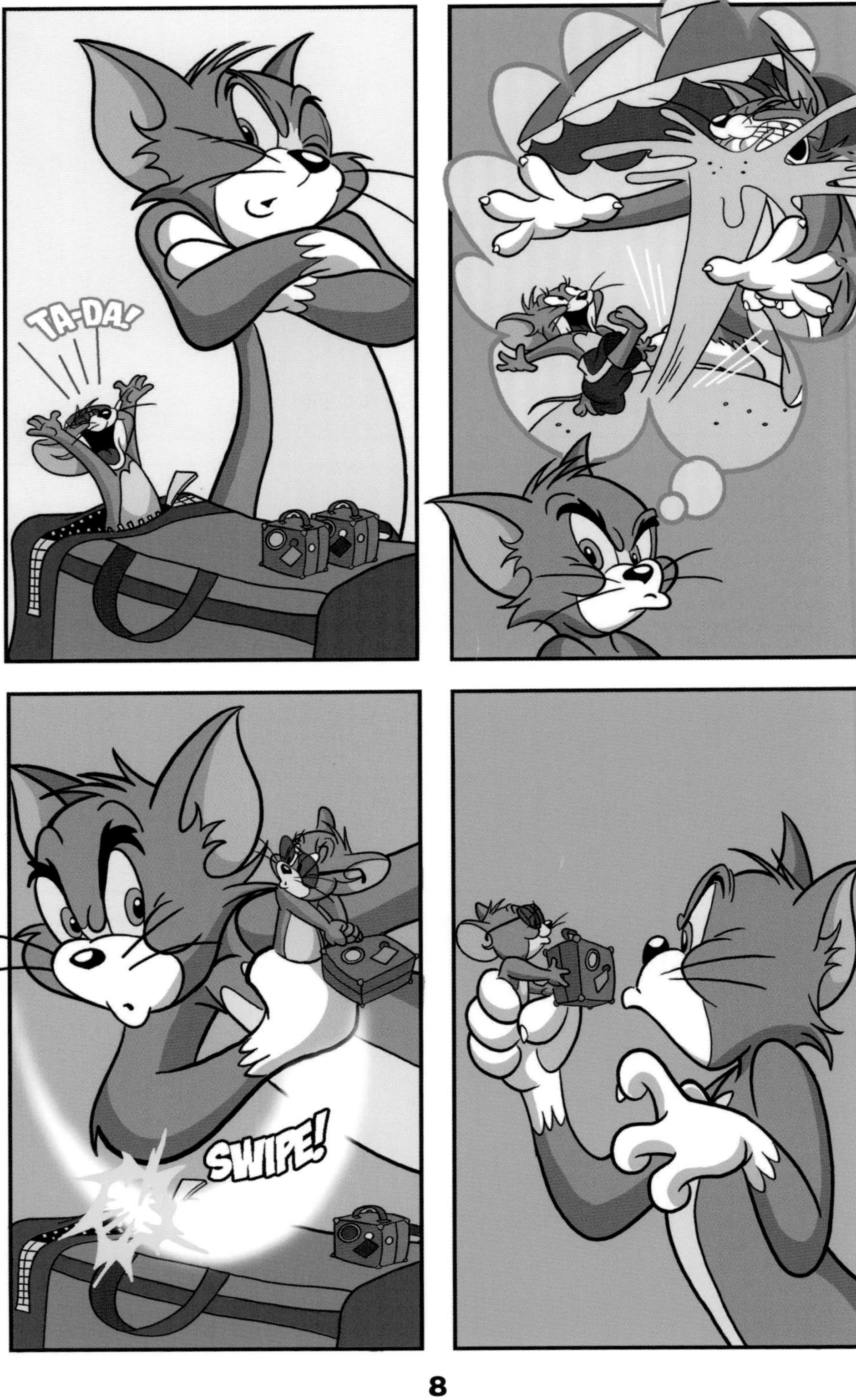
TA-DA!
SWIPE!

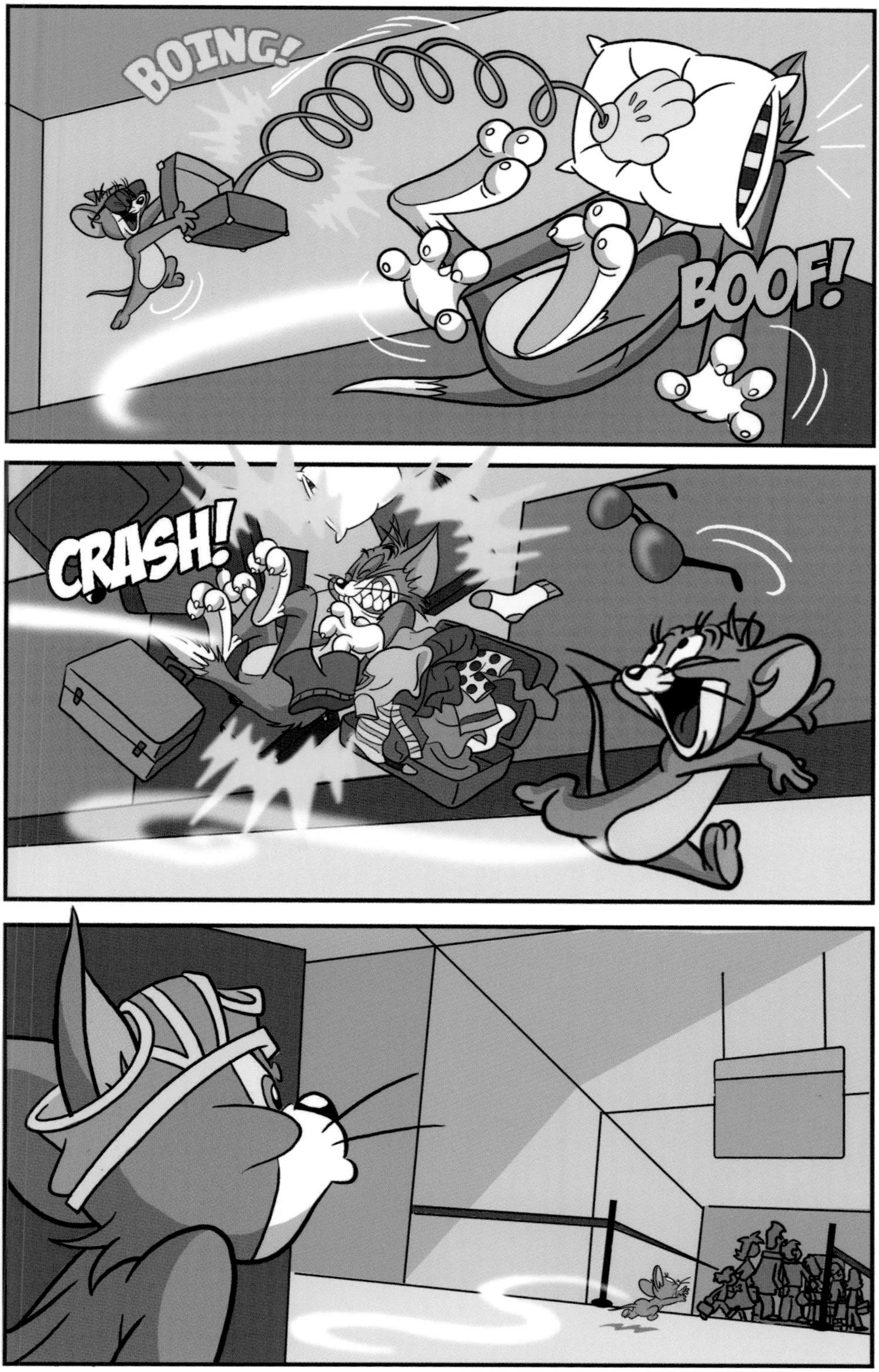
BOING!
BOOF!
CRASH!

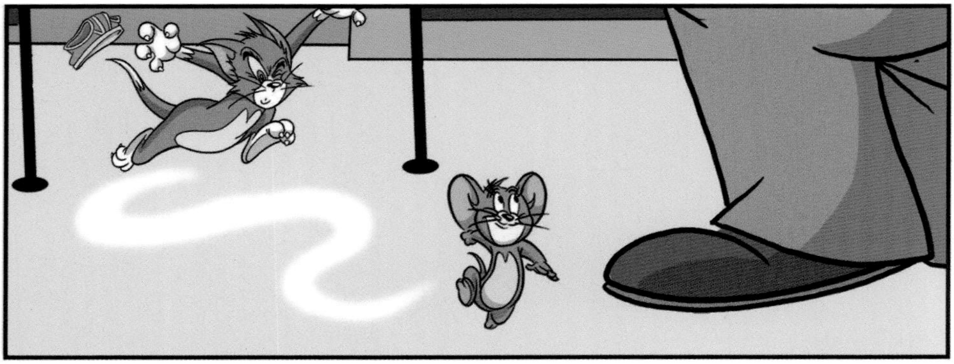

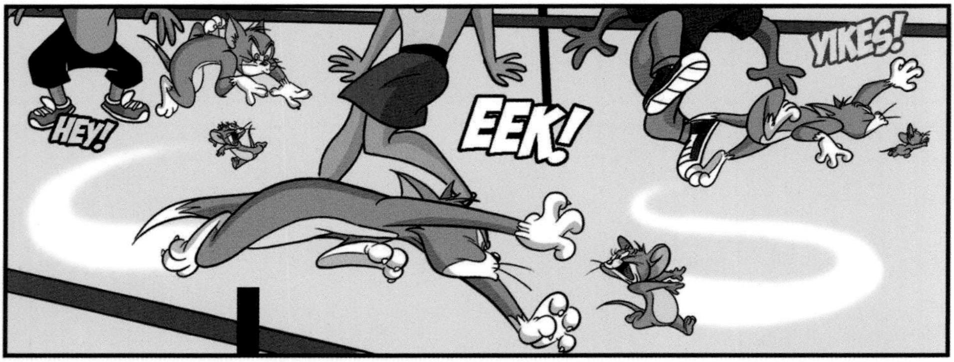
HEY!
EEK!
YIKES!

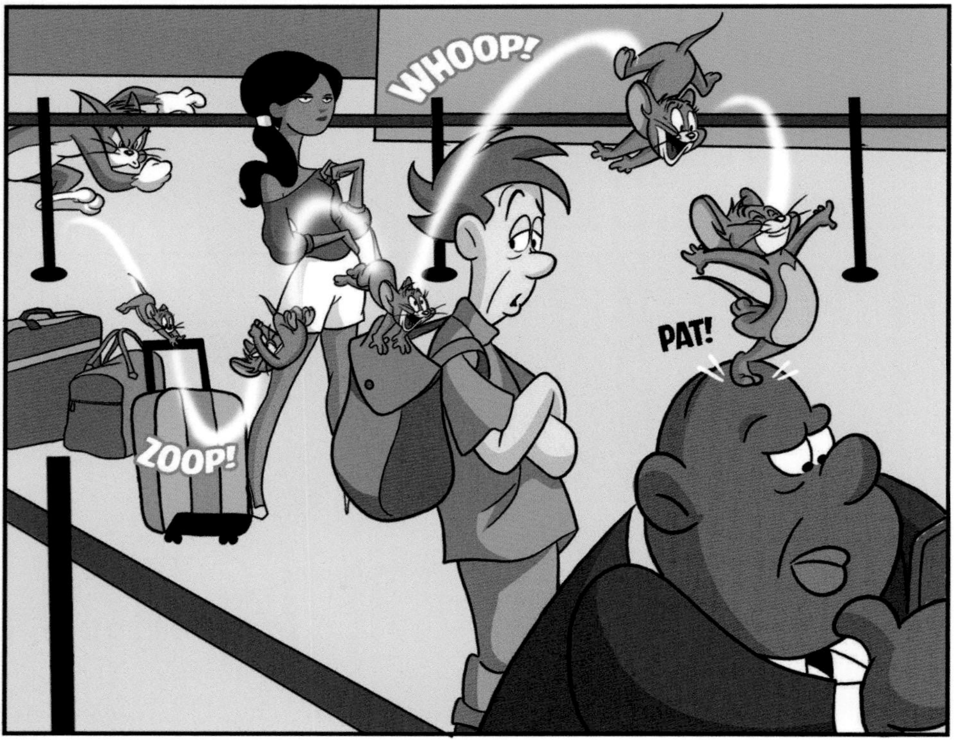
WHOOP!
ZOOP!
PAT!

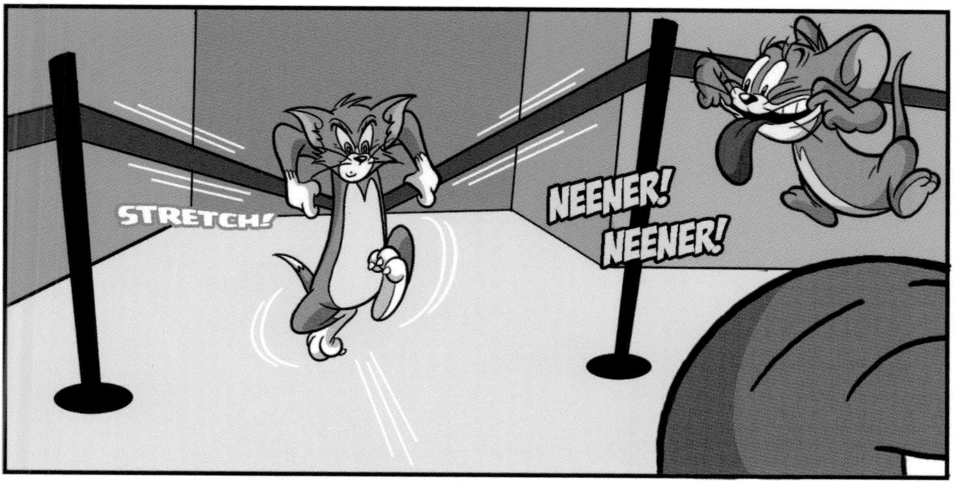
STRETCH!
NEENER! NEENER!

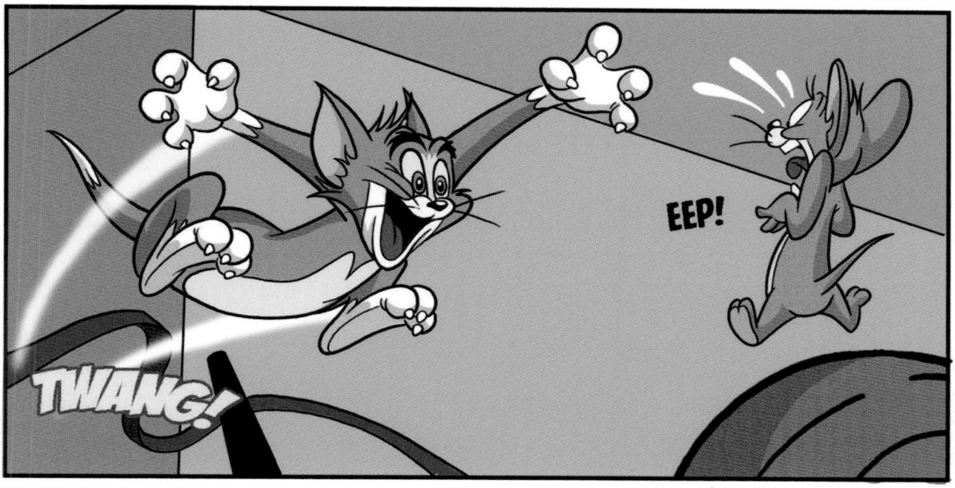
EEP!
TWANG!

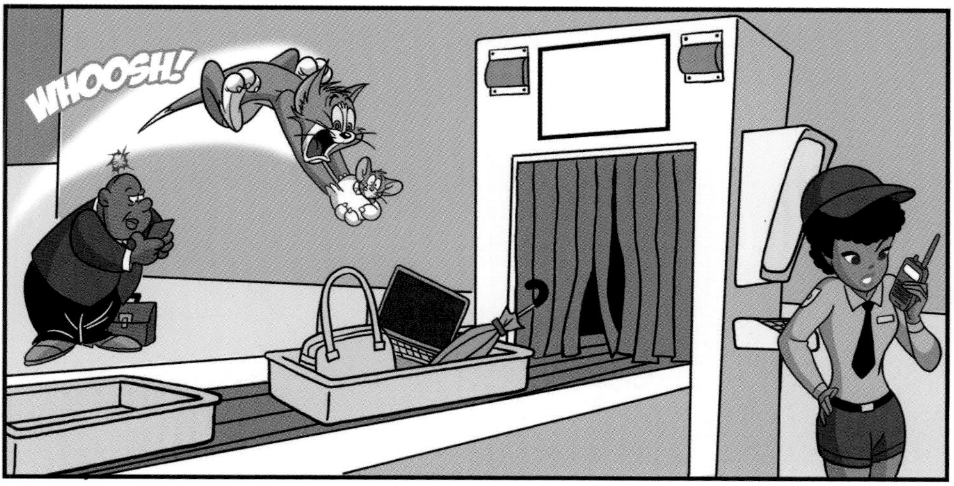
WHOOSH!

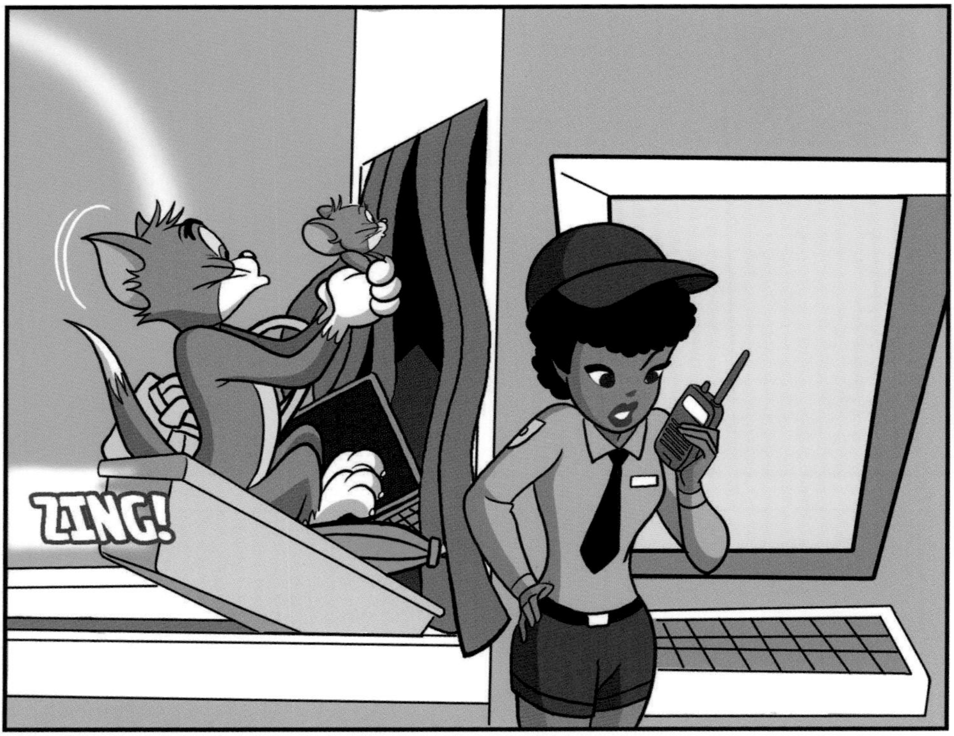
ZING!
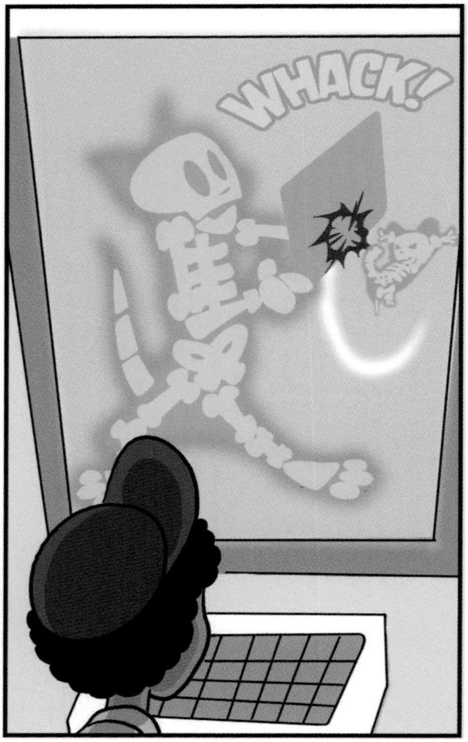
WHACK!
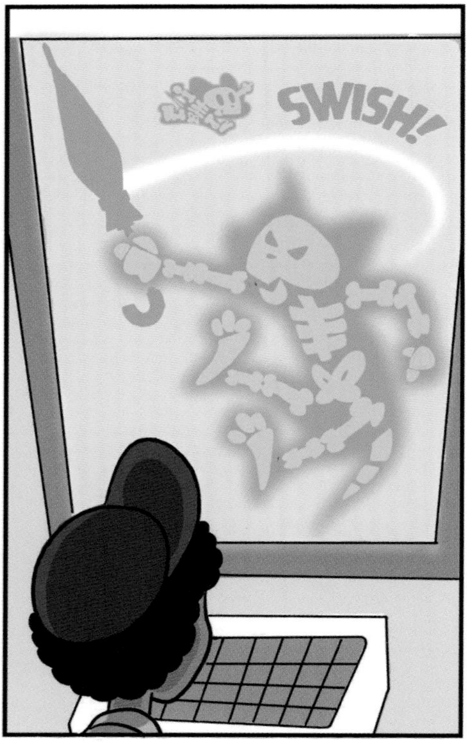
SWISH!

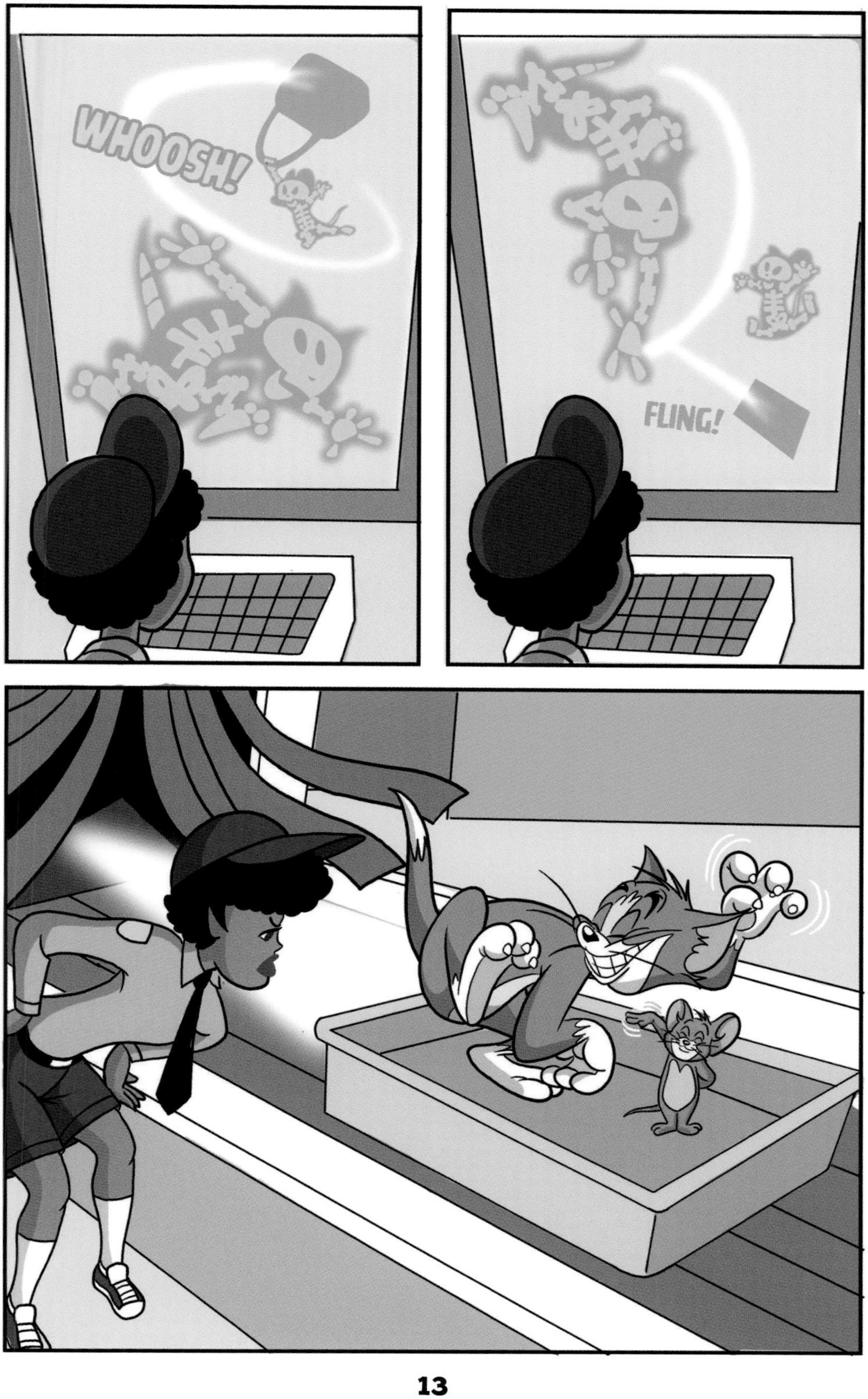
WHOOSH!
FLING!

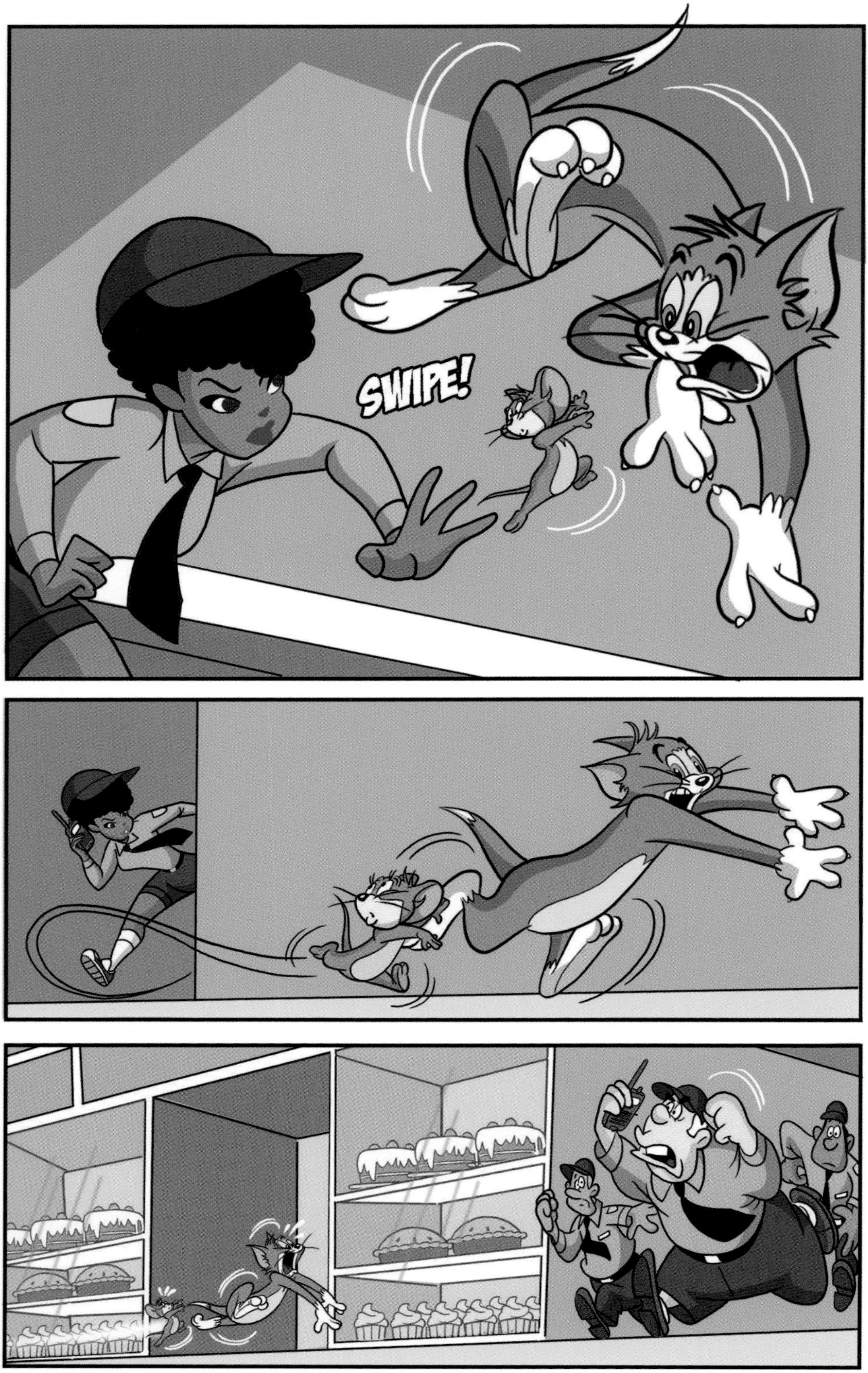
SWIPE!

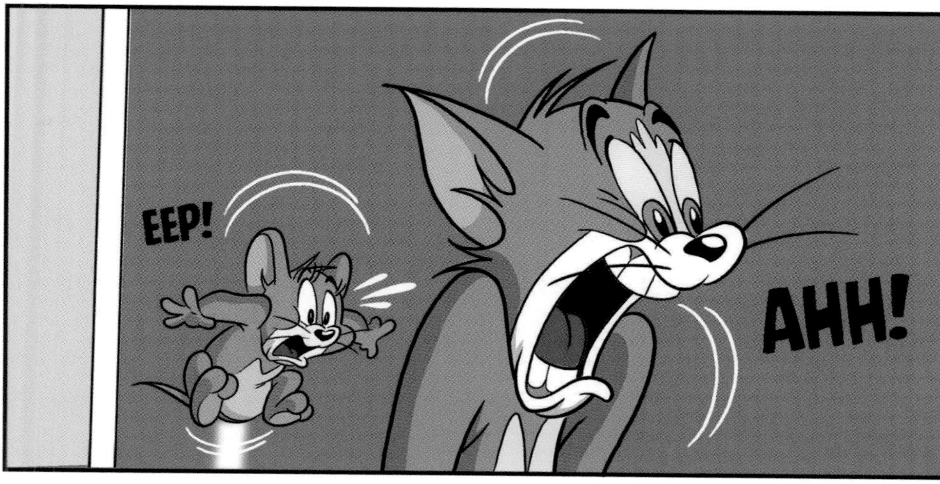
EEP!
AHH!

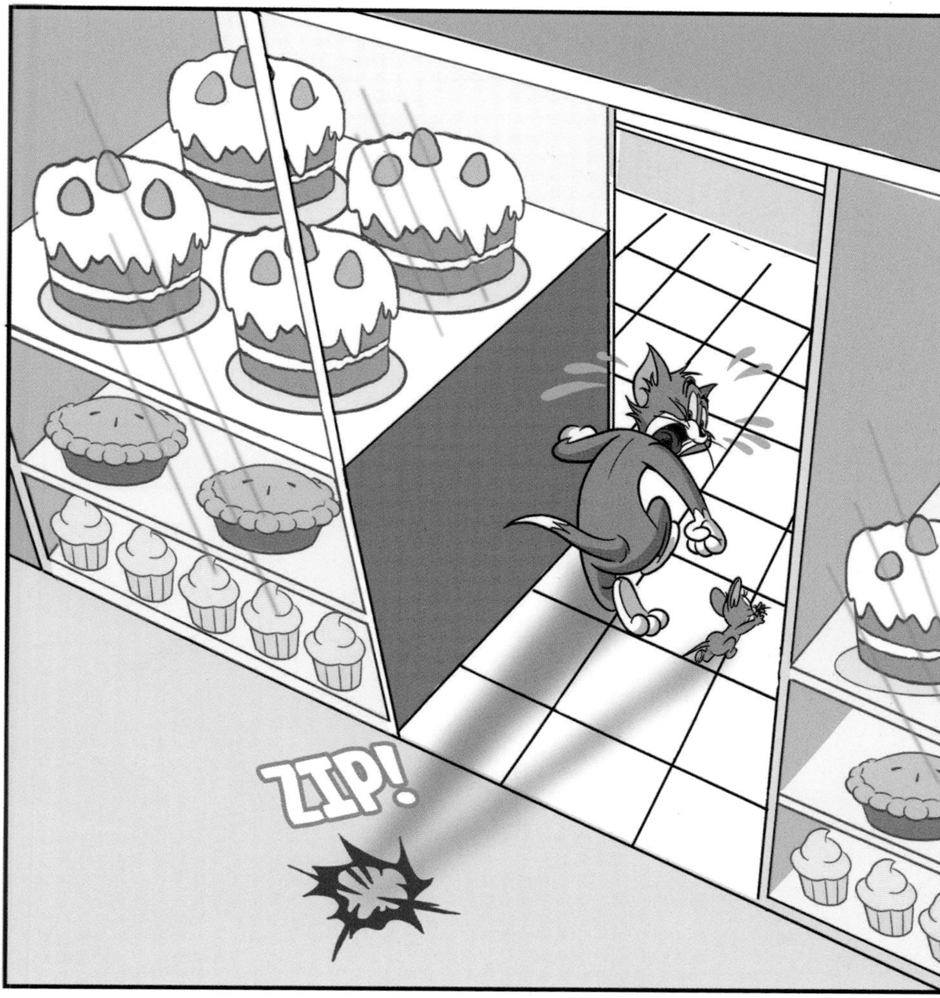
ZIP!

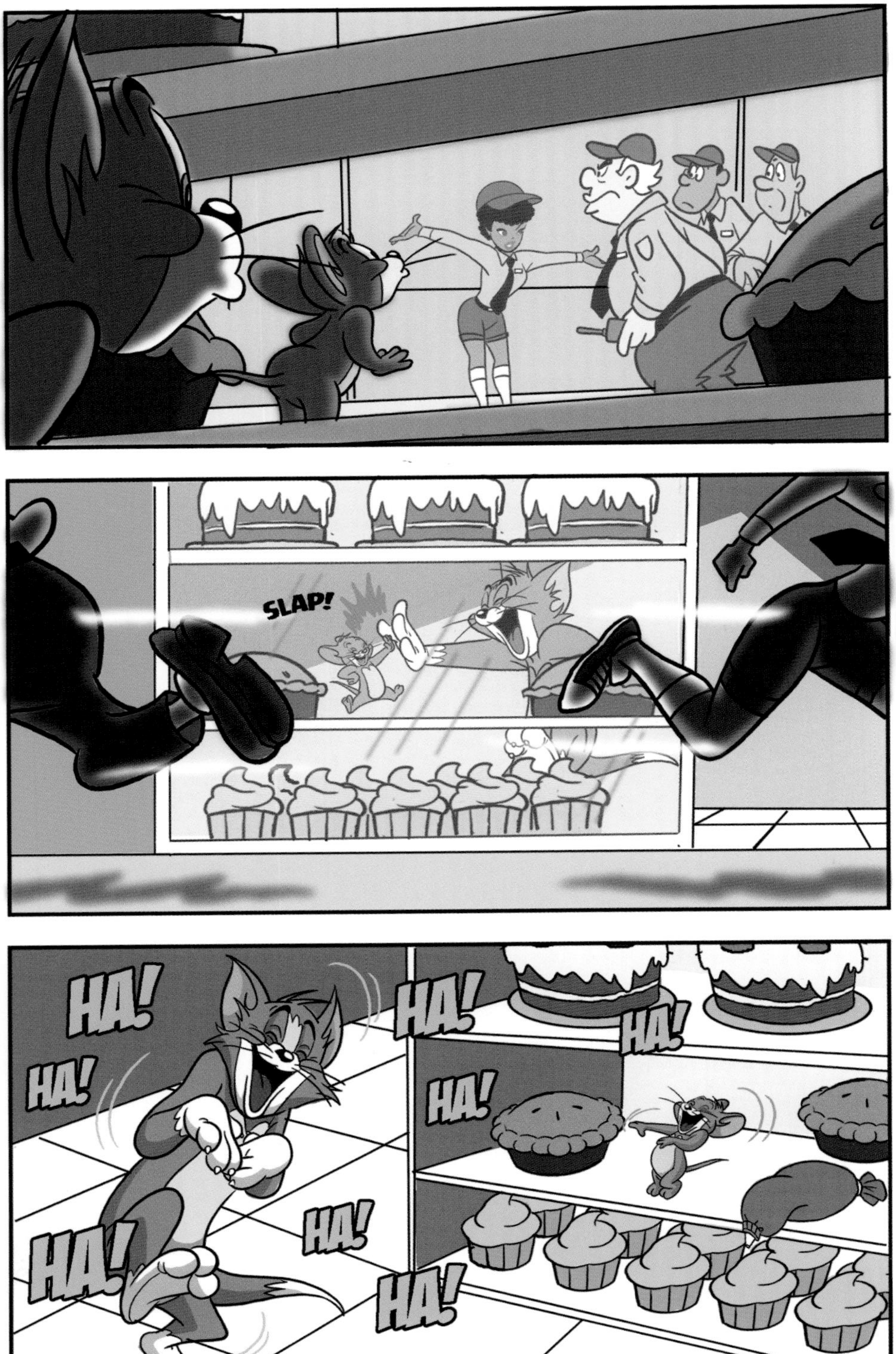
SLAP!
HA!
HA!
HA!
HA!
HA!
HA!
HA!
HA!

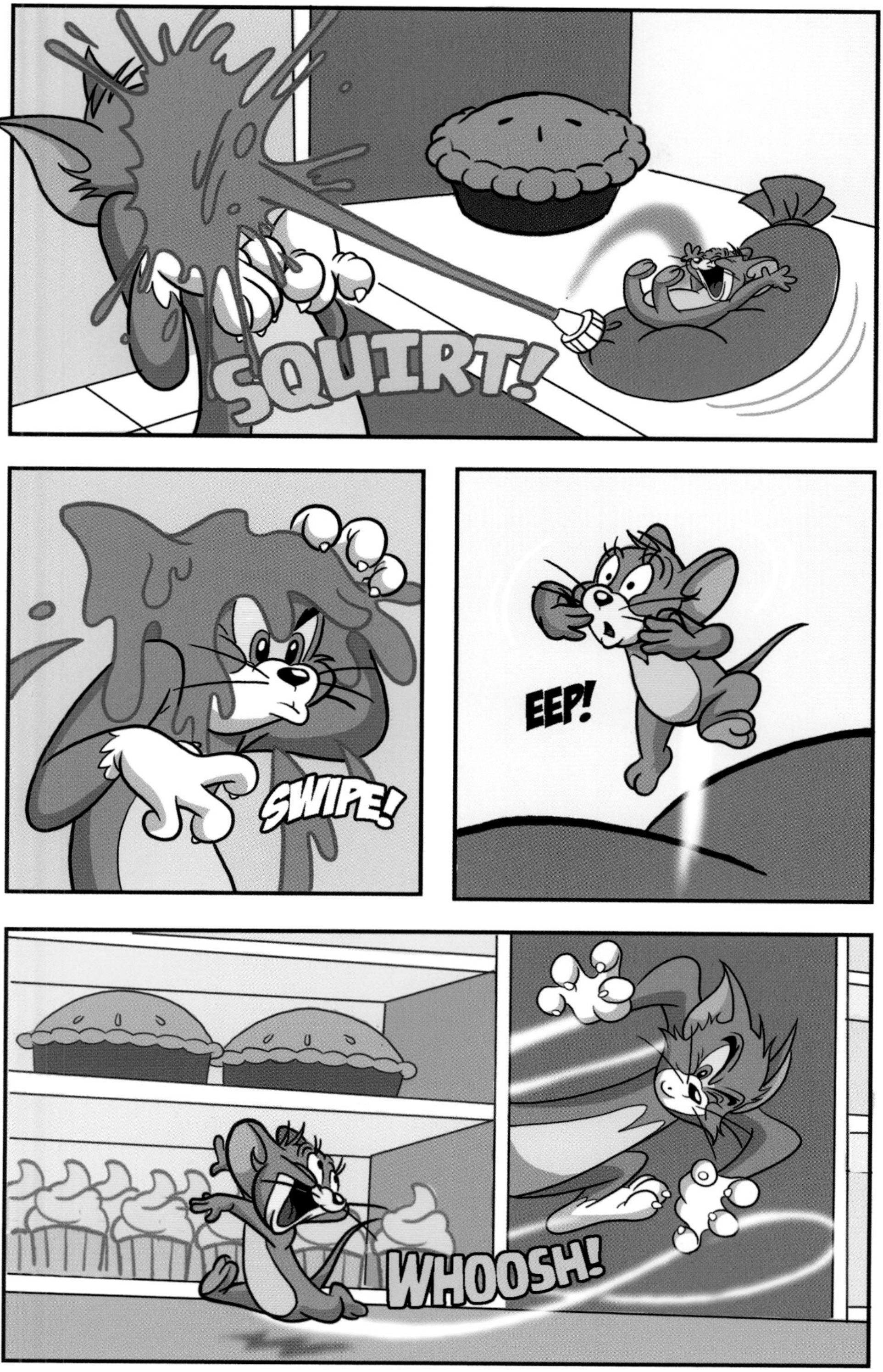
SQUIRT!
SWIPE!
EEP!
WHOOSH!

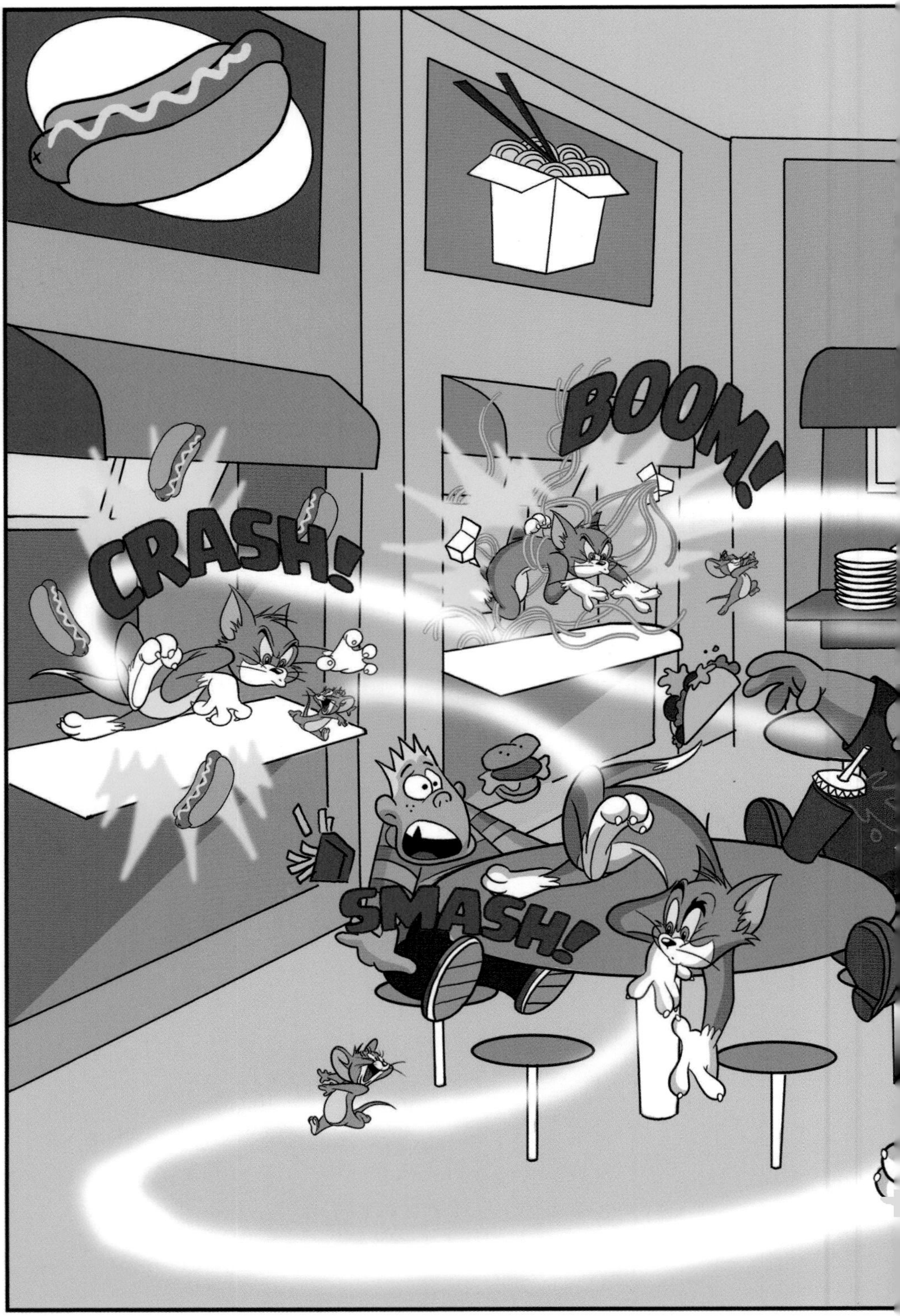
BOOM!
CRASH!
SMASH!

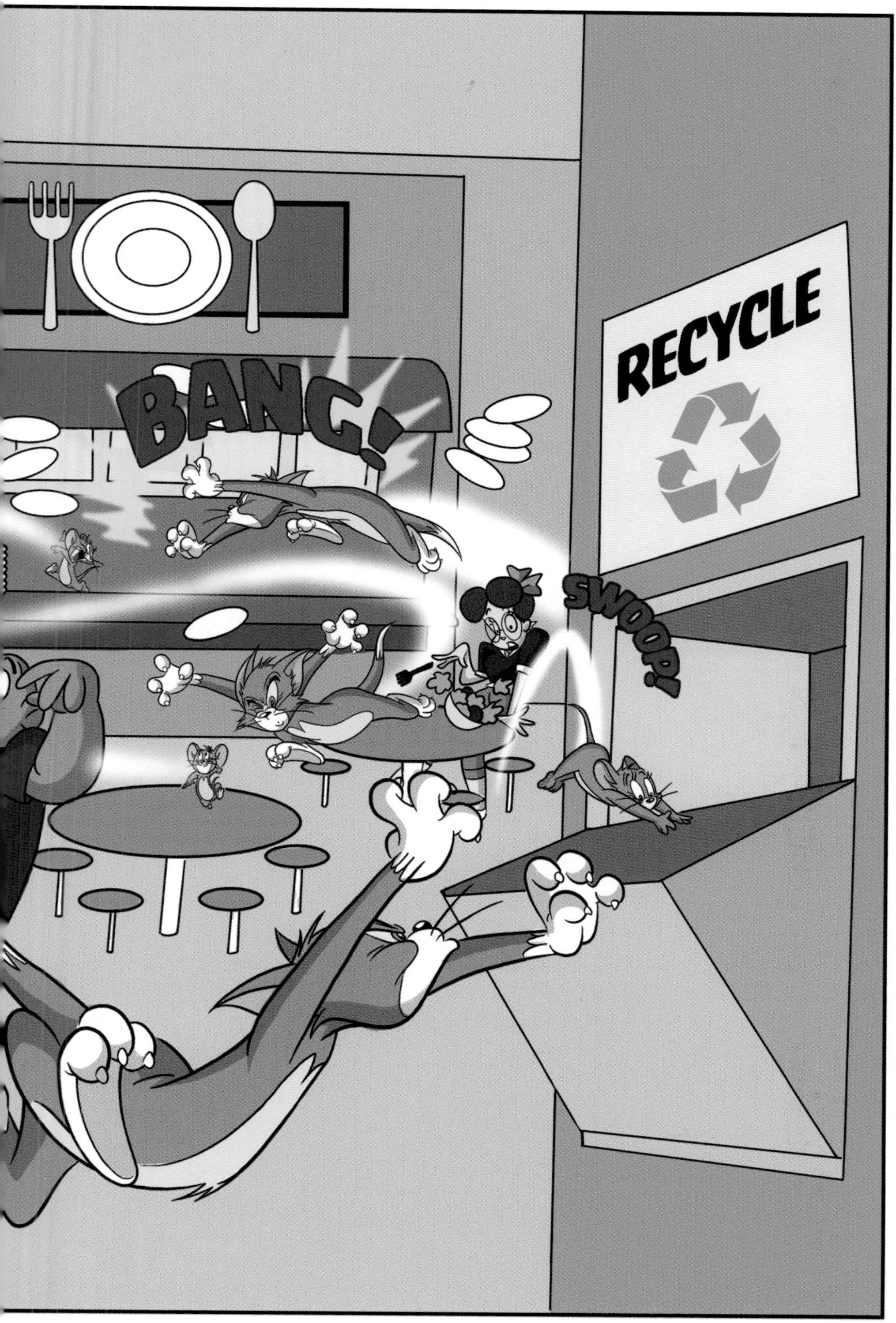
BANG!
RECYCLE
SWOOP!

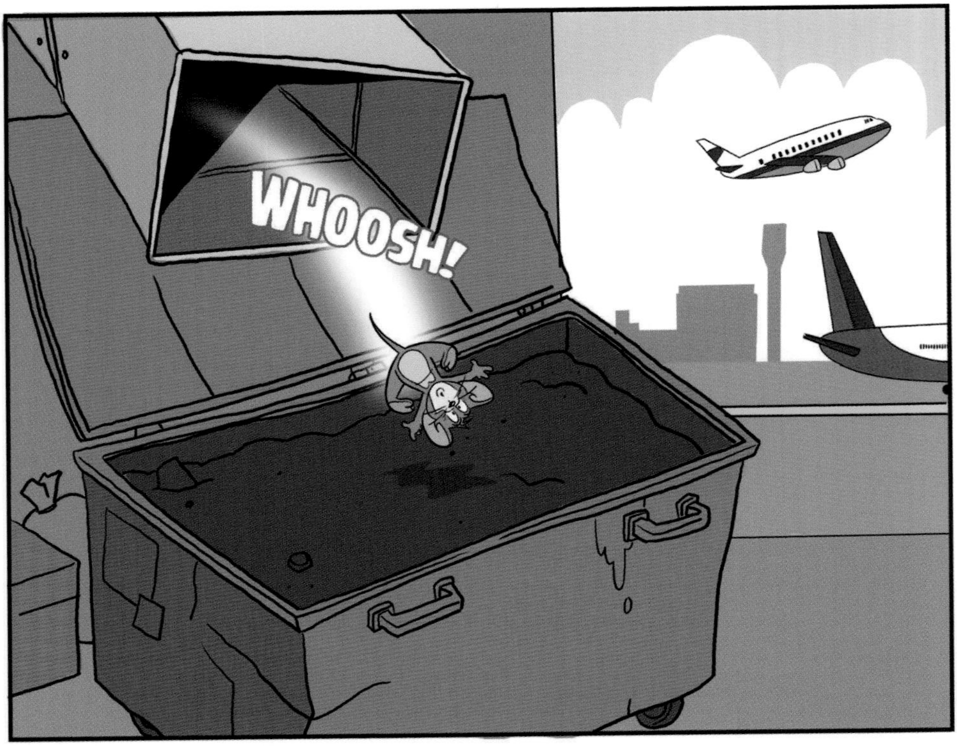
WHOOSH!

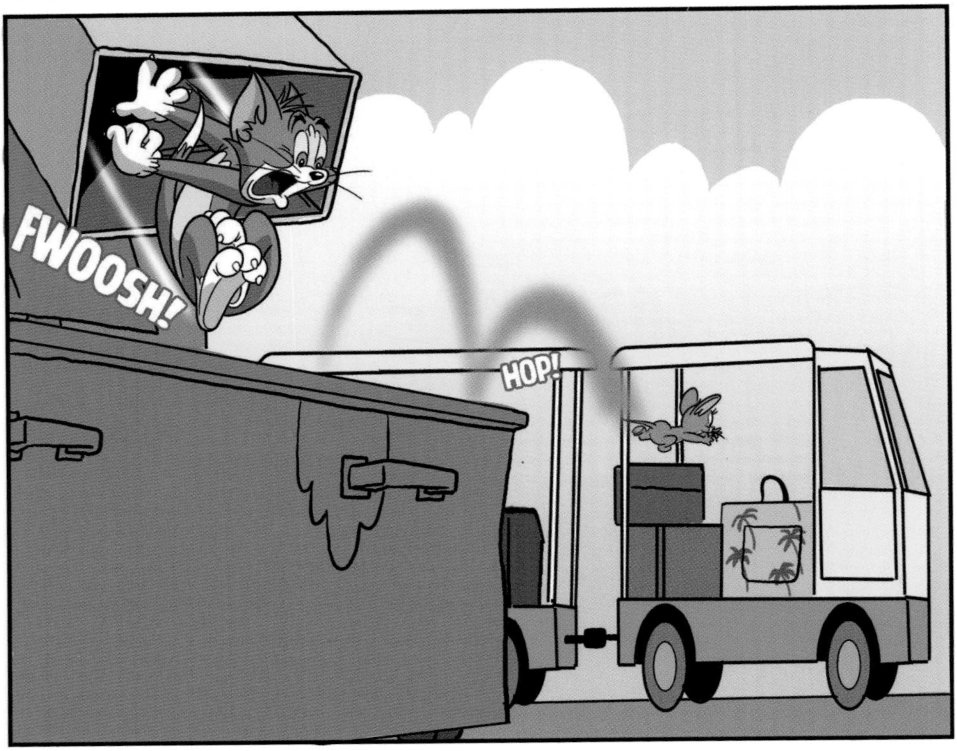
FWOOSH!
HOP!

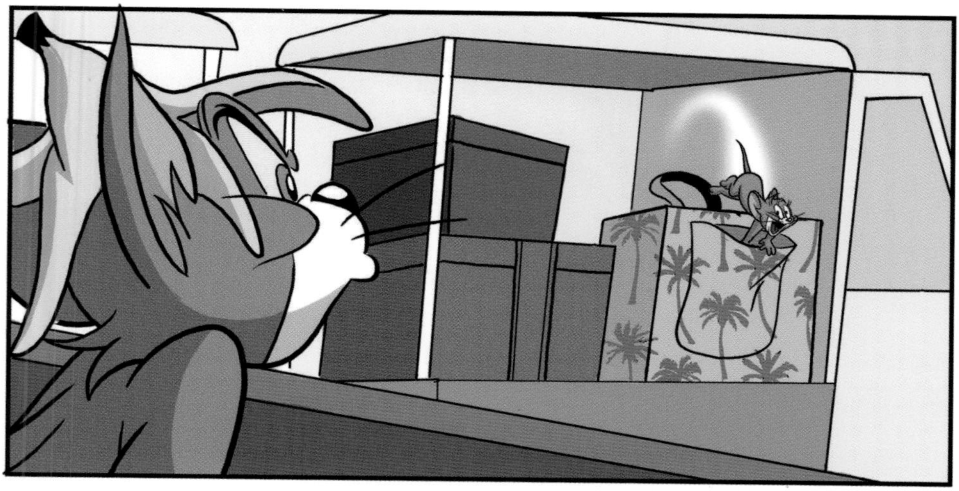

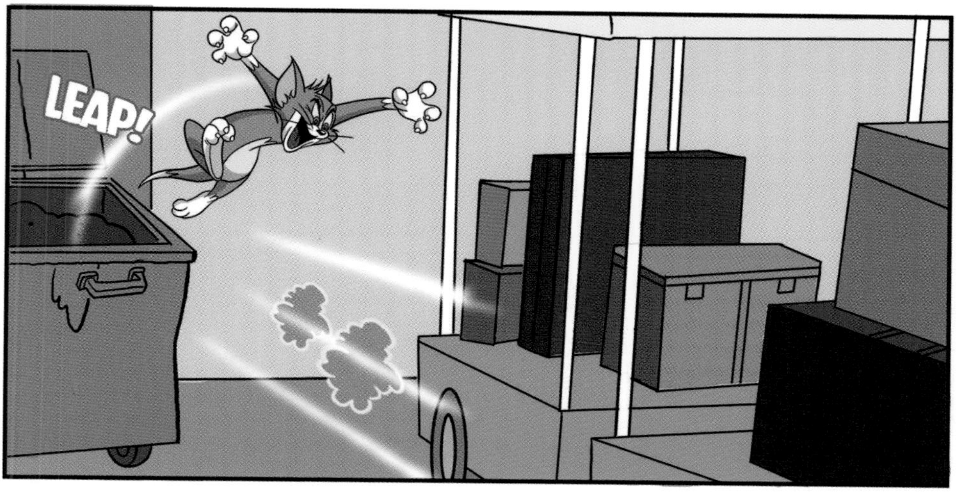
LEAP!

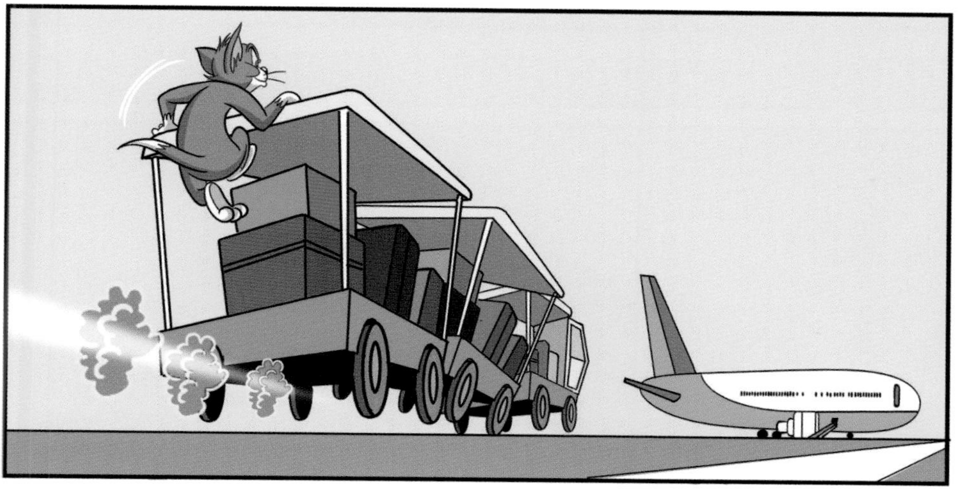

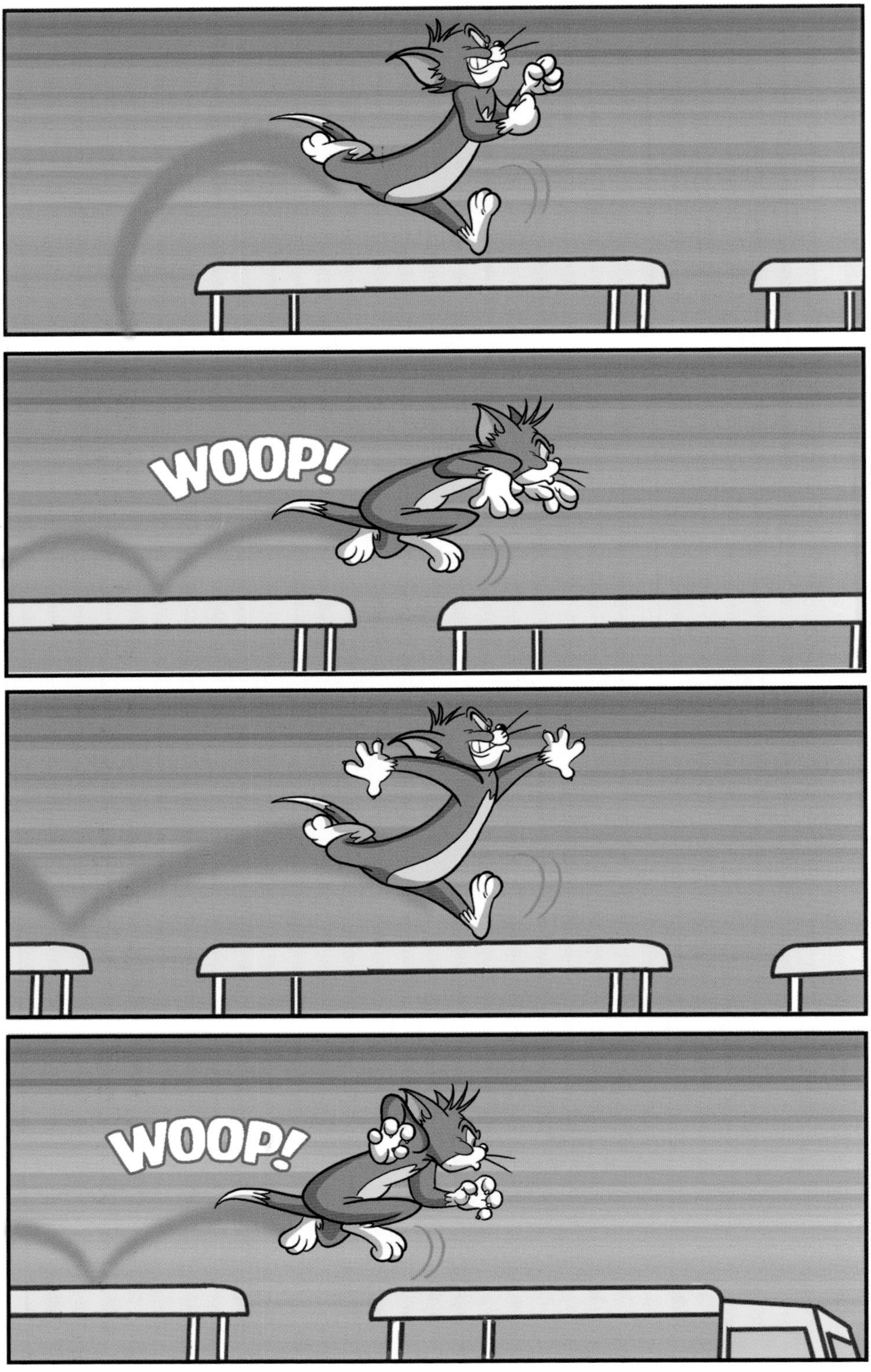
WOOP!
WOOP!

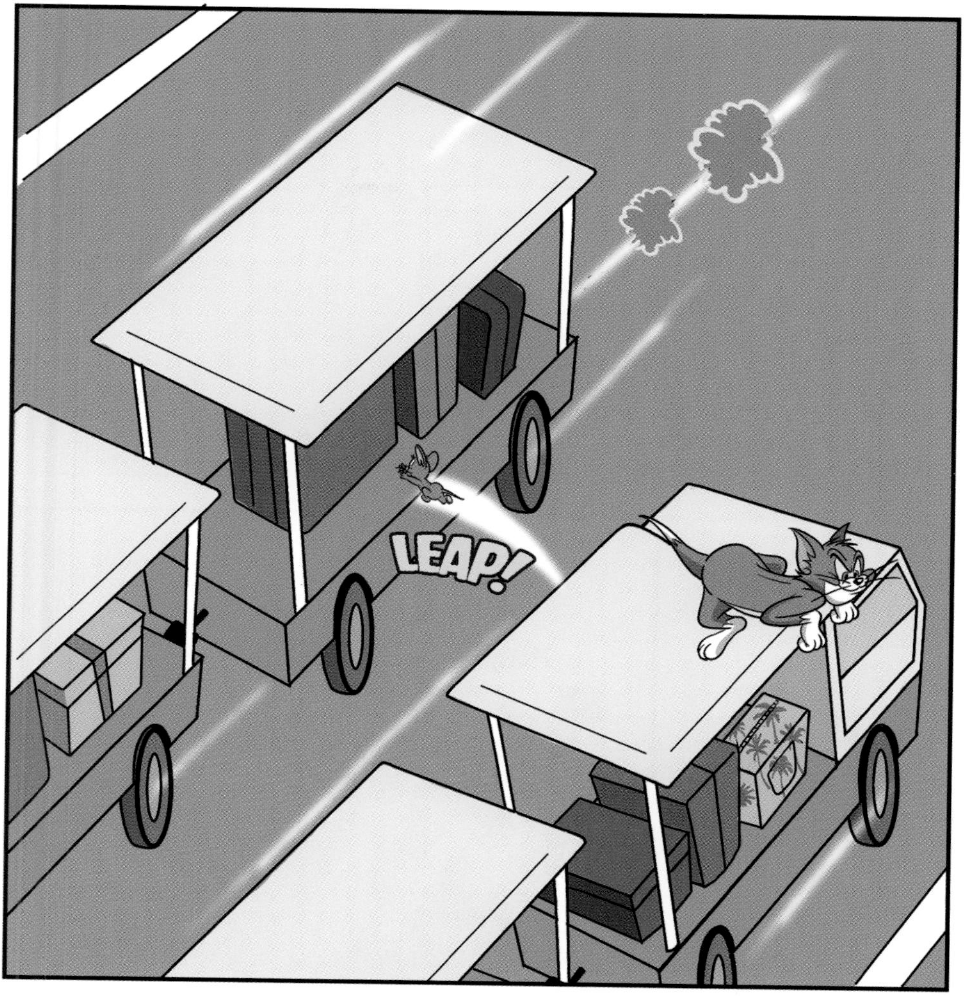
LEAP!

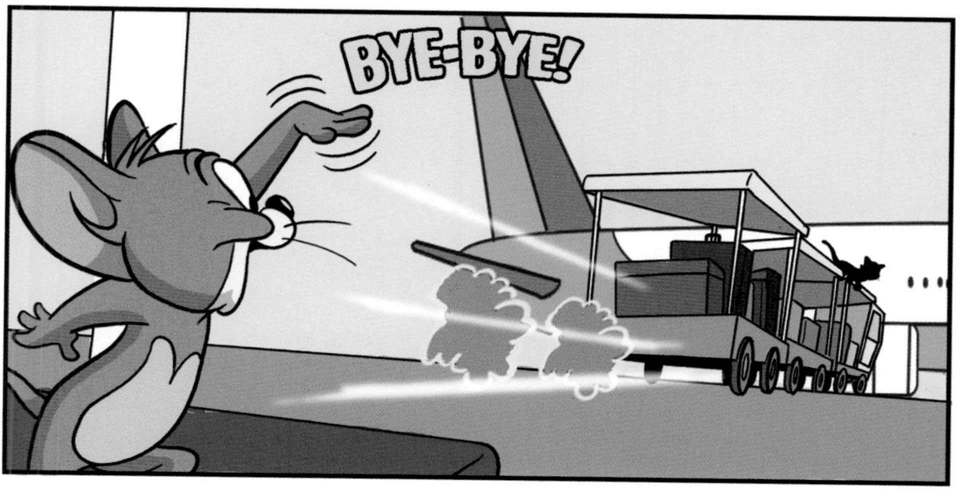
BYE-BYE!

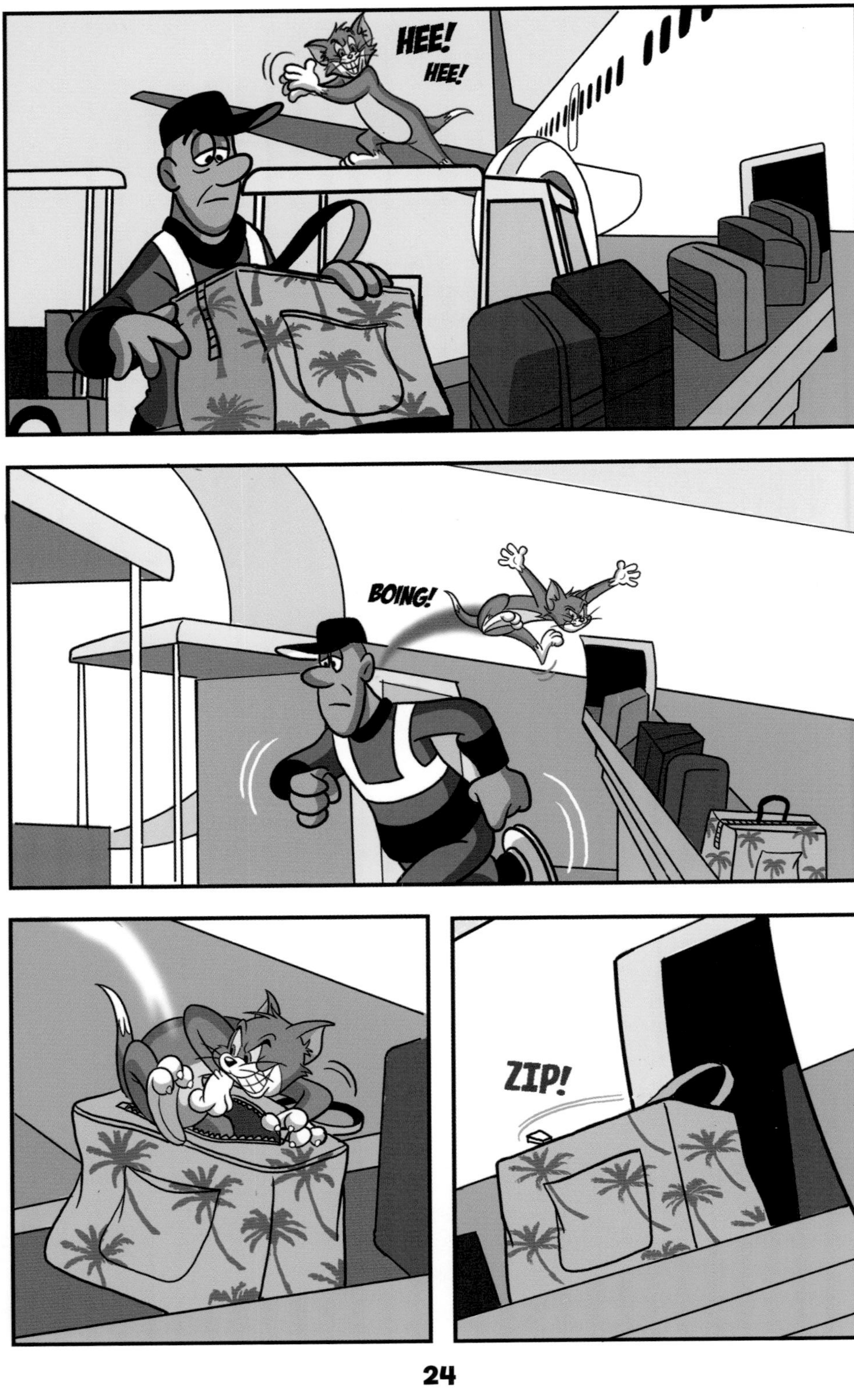
HEE!
HEE!
BOING!
ZIP!

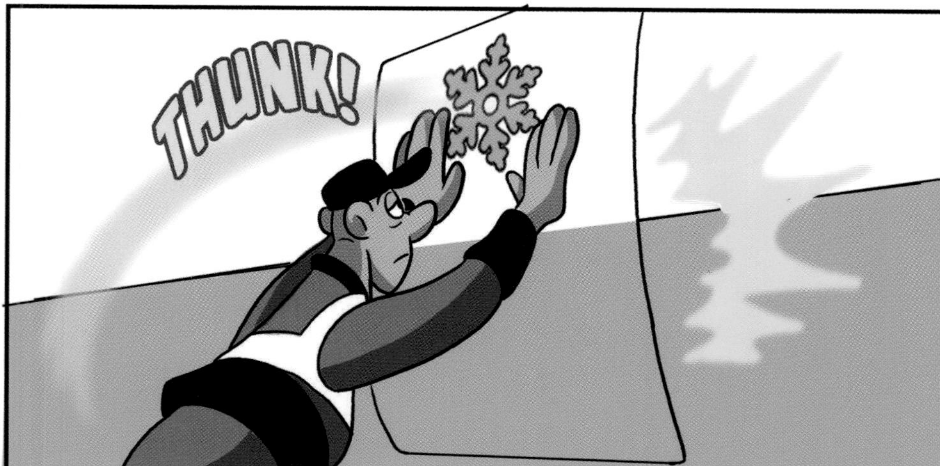
THUNK!

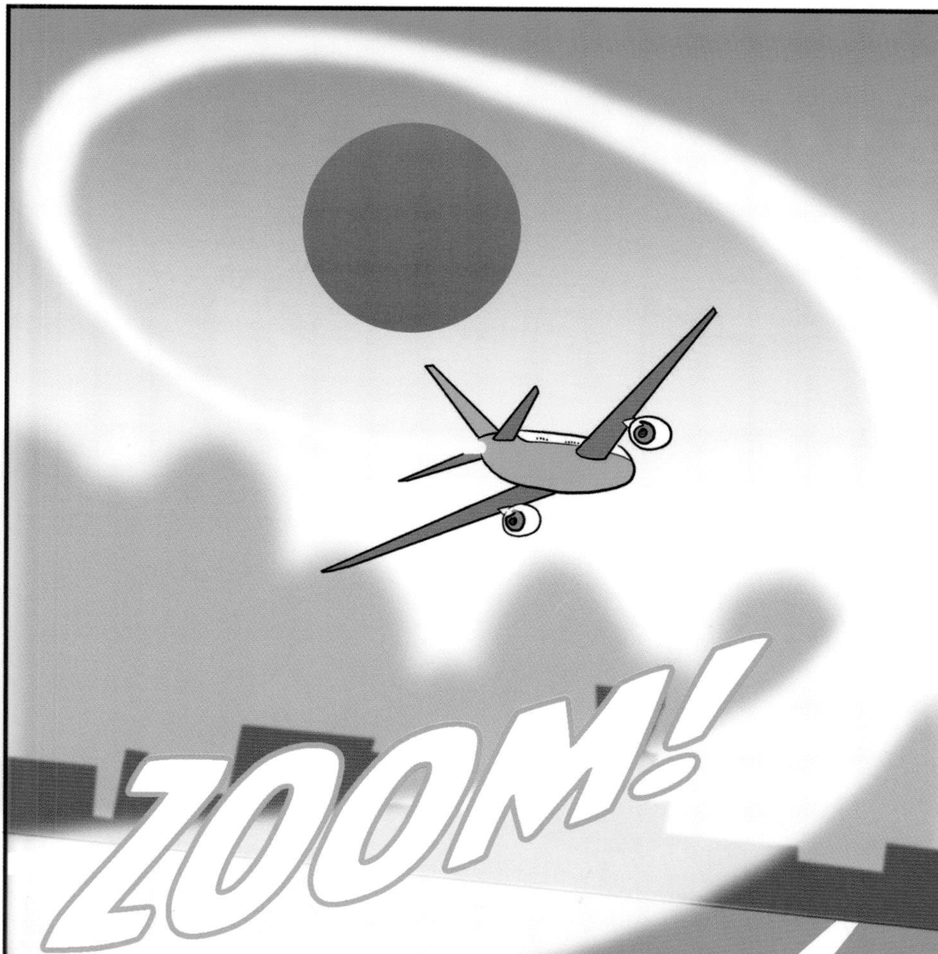
ZOOM!

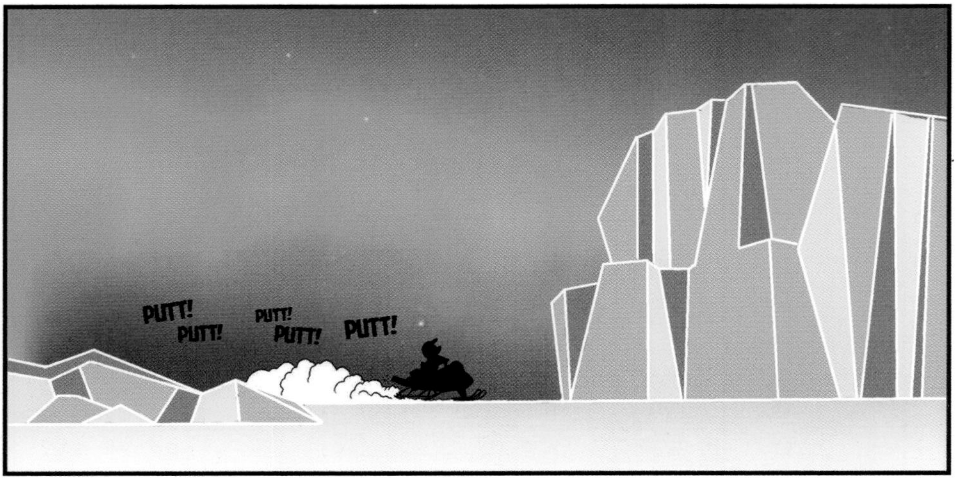
PUTT!
PUTT!
PUTT!
PUTT!
PUTT!

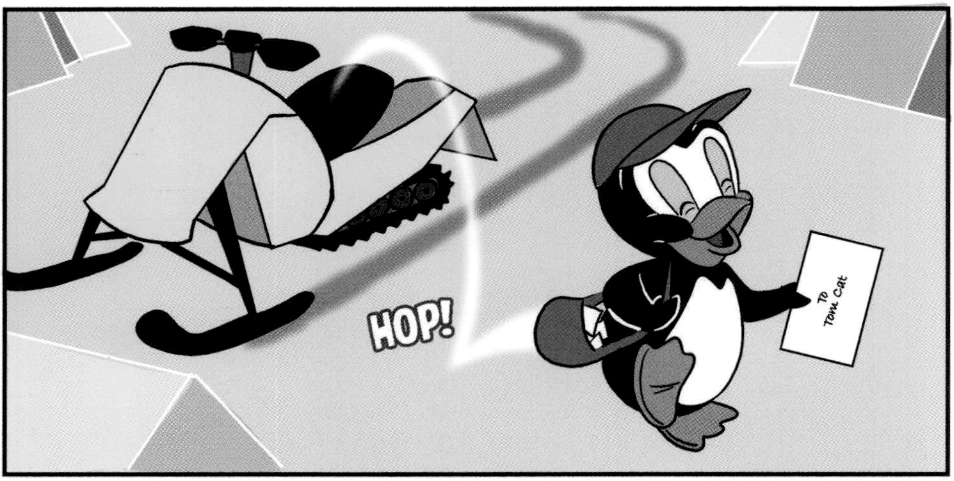
HOP!
TO TOM Cat

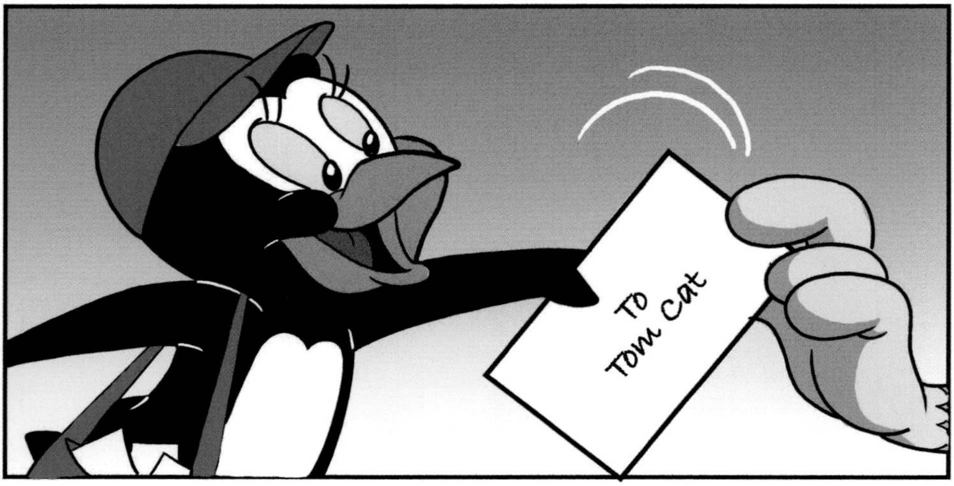
TO TOM Cat

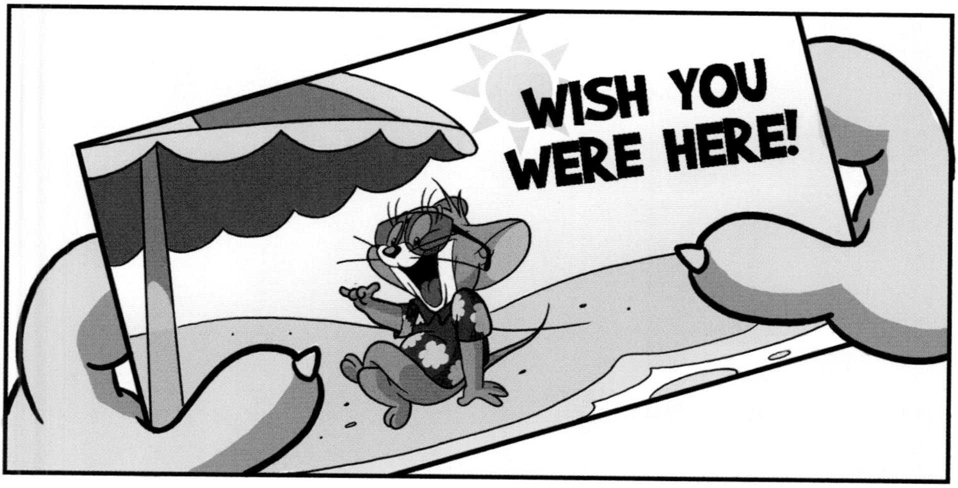
WISH YOU
WERE HERE!

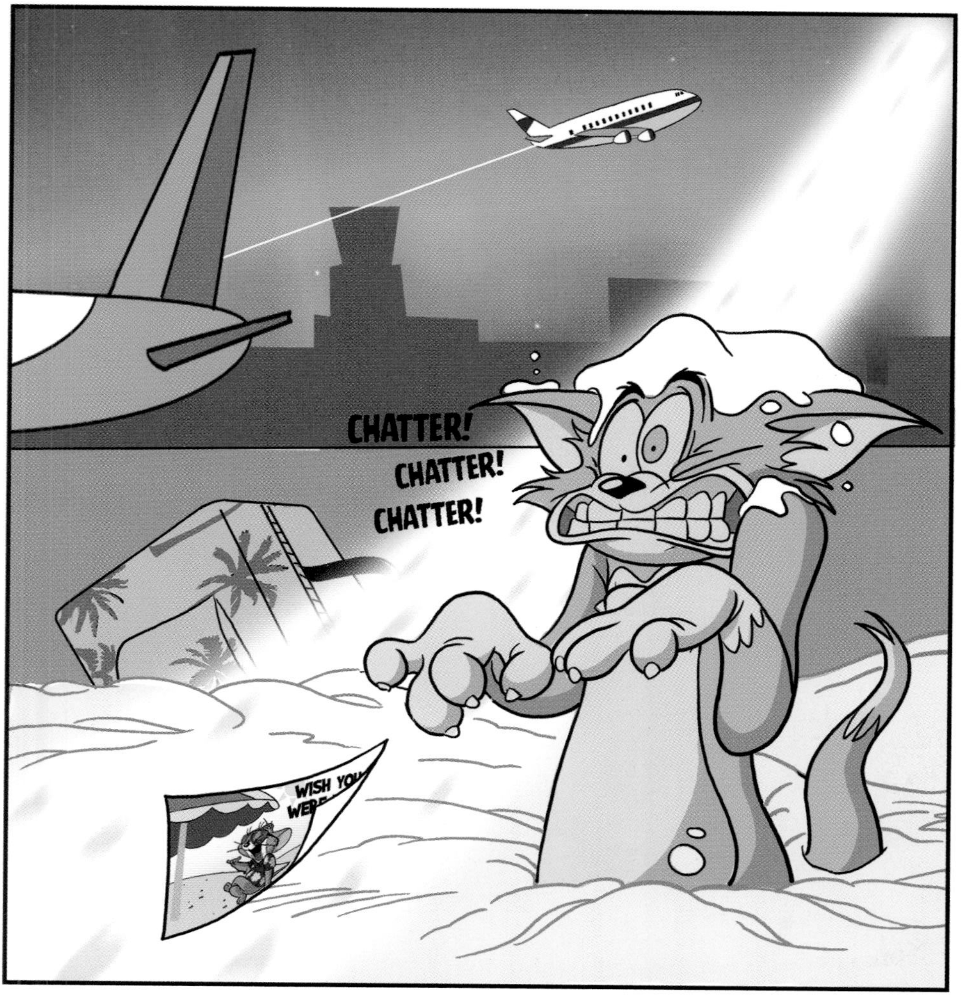
CHATTER!
CHATTER!
CHATTER!
WISH YOU

Panel Talk

1. What does Tom think will happen if Jerry tags along on his vacation? How does the look on his face help you know how he feels about that?

2. Why do Tom and Jerry share a high-five in this panel? What does it tell you about them?

3. Why does Tom hide in this suitcase? Why might he think it's the right suitcase to climb into?

4. What does Jerry's postcard tell you about where the mouse ended up at the end of the story?

WISH YOU WERE HERE!

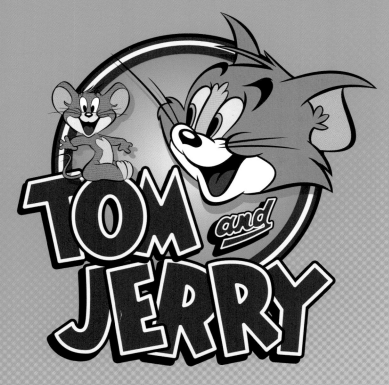

TOM and JERRY

Through the Years

Tom and Jerry have been making children (and their parents) laugh for more than 80 years. Their first short film, *Puss Gets the Boot*, hit theaters in 1940. Their animators, William Hanna and Joseph Barbera, went on to make more than 100 short films by 1957. Seven of them even won Academy Awards for Best Animated Short Subject.

After more short films in the 1960s, Tom and Jerry jumped to the small screen. Their crazy capers delighted viewers with several popular television cartoon series between the 1970s and today. And that's not all! They even made the leap back to the big screen with starring roles in feature-length movies in 1992 and 2021.

How have Tom and Jerry continued to earn countless fans through the years? By sticking to their slapstick recipe for success. Tom will stop at nothing to catch Jerry, and Jerry will always find ways to outwit Tom. After all, who can resist a rip-roaring cat-and-mouse chase?!

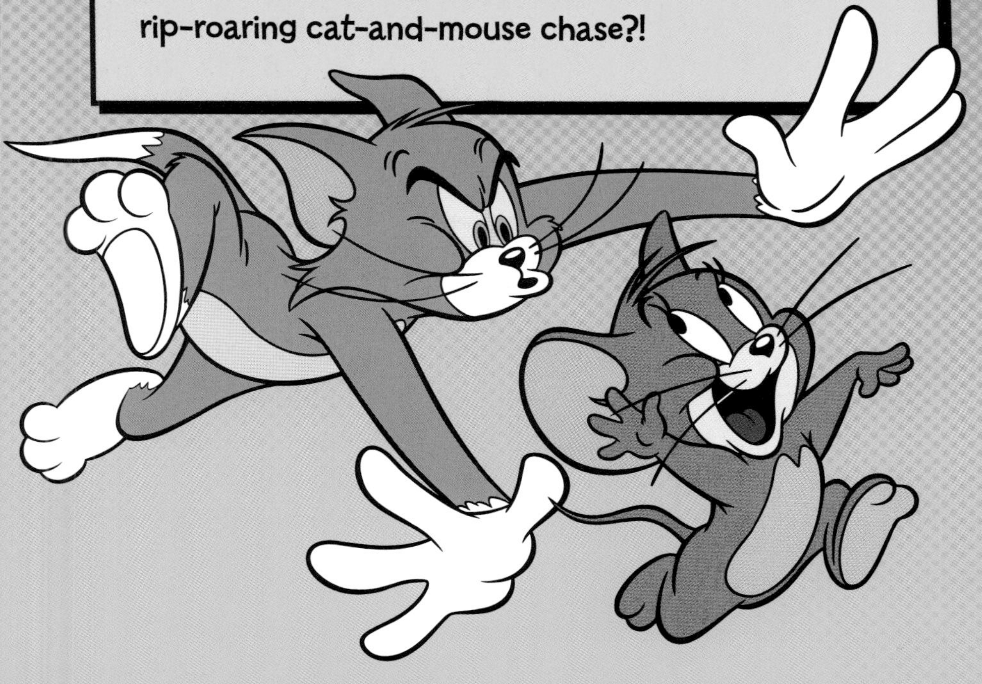

About the Author

Christopher Harbo is a children's book author and editor who loves cartoons. As a child, he spent countless hours hunkered down in front of the TV watching *Tom and Jerry*, *Scooby-Doo*, and *Super Friends*. These days, Christopher survives long Minnesota winters by watching as many cartoons as possible with his own kids. And look out, Jerry Mouse! Christopher's family has two crazy cats of their own—Newsworthy and Ninja!

About the Illustrator

Scott Jeralds has created many a smash hit, working in animation for companies including Marvel Studios, Hanna-Barbera Studios, M.G.M. Animation, Warner Bros., and Porchlight Entertainment. Scott has worked on TV series such as *The Flintstones*, *Yogi Bear*, *Scooby-Doo*, *The Jetsons*, *Krypto the Superdog*, *Tom and Jerry*, *The Pink Panther*, *Superman*, and *Secret Saturdays*, and he directed the cartoon series *Freakazoid*, for which he earned an Emmy Award. In addition, Scott has designed cartoon-related merchandise, licensing art, and artwork for several comic and children's book publications.